BASE JUMPING

By Jessica Cohn

Gareth Stevens
Publishing

Please visit our website, www.garethstevens.com. For a free color catalog of all our high-quality books, call toll free 1-800-542-2595 or fax 1-877-542-2596.

Library of Congress Cataloging-in-Publication Data

Cohn, Jessica.
 BASE jumping / Jessica Cohn.
     p. cm. — (Incredibly insane sports)
ISBN 978-1-4339-8819-6 (pbk.)
ISBN 978-1-4339-8820-2 (6-pack)
ISBN 978-1-4339-8818-9 (library binding)
1. Jumping—Juvenile literature. 2. Extreme sports—Juvenile literature. I. Title.
 GV529.C63 2013
 796.43'2—dc23

                        2012037752

First Edition
Published in 2013 by
Gareth Stevens Publishing
111 East 14th Street, Suite 349
New York, NY 10003

©2013 Gareth Stevens Publishing

Produced by Netscribes Inc.
Art Director Dibakar Acharjee
Editorial Content The Wordbench
Copy Editor Sarah Chassé
Picture Researcher Sandeep Kumar G
Designer Rishi Raj
Illustrators Ashish Tanwar, Indranil Ganguly, Prithwiraj Samat, and Rohit Sharma

Photo credits:
Page no. = #, t = top, a = above, b = below, l = left, r = right, c = center
Front Cover: Shutterstock Images LLC Title Page: Shutterstock Images LLC
Contents Page: Shutterstock Images LLC Inside: Shutterstock Images LLC: 4c, 4r, 5, 6,7t, 7b, 8, 9, 10, 11t, 11c, 12, 13, 14, 15, 16, 17, 18, 19t, 19b, 20, 21t, 21b, 22, 23, 24, 25, 26t, 26b, 27, 28, 29, 30, 31, 33, 34, 35, 36, 37, 28, 39t, 39b, 40, 41, 42, 43, 45.

Printed in the United States of America

CPSIA compliance information: Batch #CW13GS: For further information contact Gareth Stevens, New York, New York at 1-800-542-2595.

Contents

Jump to It   4
First Thoughts   10
Diving In   14
Mastering the Jump   22
Day to Remember   28
Living the Dream   38
Jump on Jargon   42
Legends of BASE Jumping   44
Glossary   46
For More Information   47
Index   48

JUMP TO IT

Each October, thousands of people gather for Bridge Day at the New River **Gorge** Bridge in West Virginia. On that day, the bridge is closed to cars, and people are allowed to walk across it. Many more people line up along the gorge to watch BASE jumpers fly off the bridge.

A Tall Fall

The jumps are stunning. The bridge is 876 feet (267 m) above the New River, so the jumpers use **parachutes** to slow them down. To picture that height, think of a building that is eight or nine stories tall. Each story in a building is about 10 feet (3 m) in height.

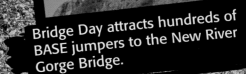

Bridge Day attracts hundreds of BASE jumpers to the New River Gorge Bridge.

Making the Jump

The people who organize the event do the best they can to make sure that the jumpers understand the dangers involved. Participants must be 18, and they need to have BASE training that includes recent jumps. To leap from that height safely, they have just eight seconds to open their parachutes and land.

Action movies often feature BASE jumping from skyscrapers, cliffs, and other tall objects.

5

The dangers in BASE jumping include faulty parachutes and human error.

Leap of Faith

If a fall from 876 feet (267 m) sounds dangerous, that's because it is. BASE jumping is extremely risky, and the people who pursue this sport do so knowing they are in danger of dying. At Bridge Day, 71 percent of jumpers land on the shore of the river below. Twenty-eight percent land in water. The rest end up in trees and elsewhere, and some are injured.

To the Letter

BASE jumping is related to skydiving, except skydivers jump from planes. A BASE jumper flies from the top of a giant **fixed object**. BASE stands for "Building, **Antenna**, **Span**, Earth." These are the four kinds of structures used in this extreme sport.

Sometimes, the name BASE appears as B.A.S.E.

Natural Attractions

Angel Falls in South America is popular with BASE jumpers. It is the world's tallest waterfall, so it attracts jumpers for natural reasons. People go for the beauty of the falls and also because there is a clear area below, and safe landings are possible. Another popular spot is Kjerag, a huge cliff in Norway. It attracts jumpers from all over the world for the same reasons.

Wrong Way

Bridge Day is popular because it is hard to find spots for jumping in the United States. This is especially true in cities and other areas where people could be hurt below. For example, BASE jumpers have jumped from the Gateway Arch in St. Louis, Missouri. But leaping from there is against the law, and the people who did either died or were arrested. U.S. officials used to allow BASE jumping in national parks, but now they forbid it.

In 1980, someone jumped from a plane to the top of the Gateway Arch. His plan was to BASE jump from there, but he did not survive.

TEST IT!

Grab a pencil, a ruler, and paper and try to draw a structure that might be safe for a BASE jump.

Height and time: From 500 feet (152 m) without a parachute, a jumper has about 5 seconds before hitting the ground. From 500 feet with an open parachute, the jumper has about 12 seconds.

Other considerations: Is there a place to land? Does the base of the structure jut into the landing space? What happens if it is windy?

FIRST THOUGHTS

People started dreaming of jumping and flying through the air long before there were airplanes or skyscrapers. Ancient writings from China and the Middle East mention objects that could have been parachutes. In the 15th century, Leonardo da Vinci drew pictures of a cloth held up by a **pyramid** of poles. This famous inventor and artist was one of the first people in Europe to dream of parachutes.

The Chinese started using parachutes with hard frames in the 1100s.

Four Forever

BASE jumping came about in the 1970s. People had long been parachuting off tall structures, but that is when a group of jumpers, led by Carl Boenish, started diving from four kinds of structures as proof of their skills. With these first jumps—from buildings, antennas, spans such as bridges, and earth formations—BASE jumping was born.

The first person to make all four jumps was an American named Phil Smith. He is forever known as BASE 1. Today, there is a BASE 1,500 and even higher. Each new person who makes all four jumps is given the next number.

The first BASE jumpers considered using the term BEST jumping instead. BEST stood for "Building, Earth, Span, Tower."

11

Taking the Dare

The first soft, folding parachutes were made in the late 1700s. They were open from the start, rather than opening after the leap. The equipment was improved in the early 1900s, during World War I. The first troops supplied with parachutes were the lookouts who rode on observation balloons. Then, the equipment was given to airplane pilots.

In the 1970s, Boenish and his friends experimented with parachutes at El Capitan, a giant rock formation in Yosemite National Park. Boenish was the first person to adapt skydiving gear to BASE jumping. Today, he is considered the father of the sport.

The CN Tower in Toronto, Canada, is one of the world's tallest free-standing structures. It is more than 1,815 feet (553 m) high.

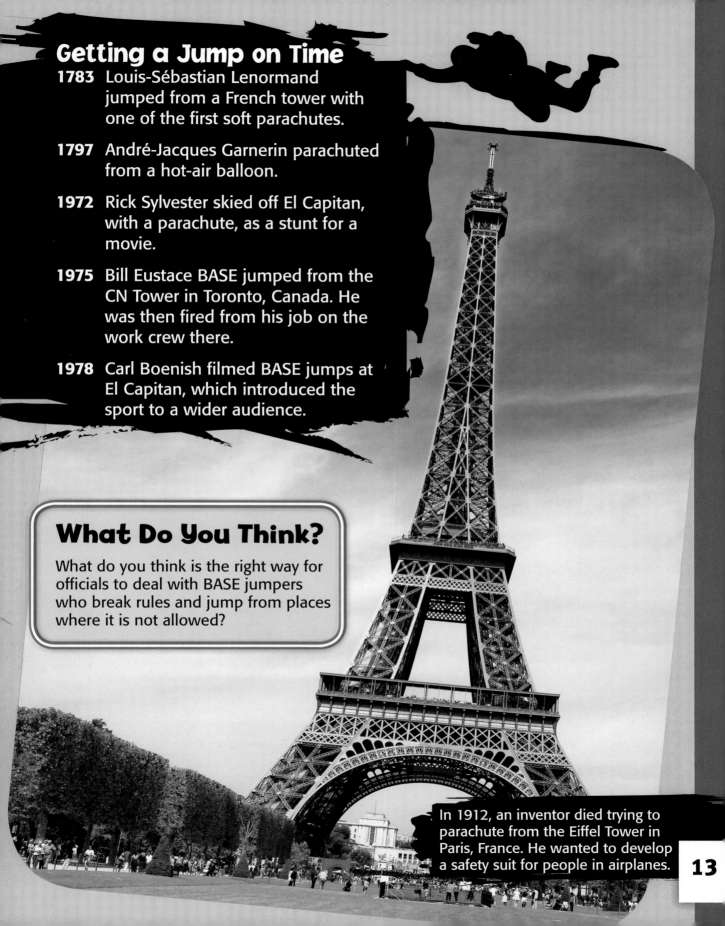

Getting a Jump on Time

1783 Louis-Sébastian Lenormand jumped from a French tower with one of the first soft parachutes.

1797 André-Jacques Garnerin parachuted from a hot-air balloon.

1972 Rick Sylvester skied off El Capitan, with a parachute, as a stunt for a movie.

1975 Bill Eustace BASE jumped from the CN Tower in Toronto, Canada. He was then fired from his job on the work crew there.

1978 Carl Boenish filmed BASE jumps at El Capitan, which introduced the sport to a wider audience.

What Do You Think?

What do you think is the right way for officials to deal with BASE jumpers who break rules and jump from places where it is not allowed?

In 1912, an inventor died trying to parachute from the Eiffel Tower in Paris, France. He wanted to develop a safety suit for people in airplanes.

13

DIVING IN

BASE jumping is like skydiving in basic ways, but it is even more dangerous. Compared with skydiving, a BASE jump starts lower to the ground. This means there is less time for the parachute to work. BASE jumping also happens close to the structure that holds the jumper. The space the jumper falls through is tight.

BASE jumping is an expensive sport. Participants must pay for travel and equipment.

In BASE jumping, as in every extreme sport, checking the gear is an extremely important safety step.

Die in the Sky

It is estimated that 1 in every 2,300 jumps results in a death. But that fact does not scare off the people determined to try it. People who want to be BASE jumpers learn to skydive first. They first take classes for skydiving and then get the special training needed to learn to use the BASE jumping equipment. After the training, new BASE jumpers look for people who are experienced to help them start out.

BASE Equipped

To pack for these high adventures, the main item needed is the parachute. The **canopy** is the tentlike part of the parachute. BASE canopies are rounded on the upper surface. This allows air to flow over them and reduces the effects of **drag**.

BASE jumpers use ram-air parachutes. Ram air is the air that enters the chute at high speeds. Its pressure increases during the jump. The rectangular shape of the chutes makes full use of ram air.

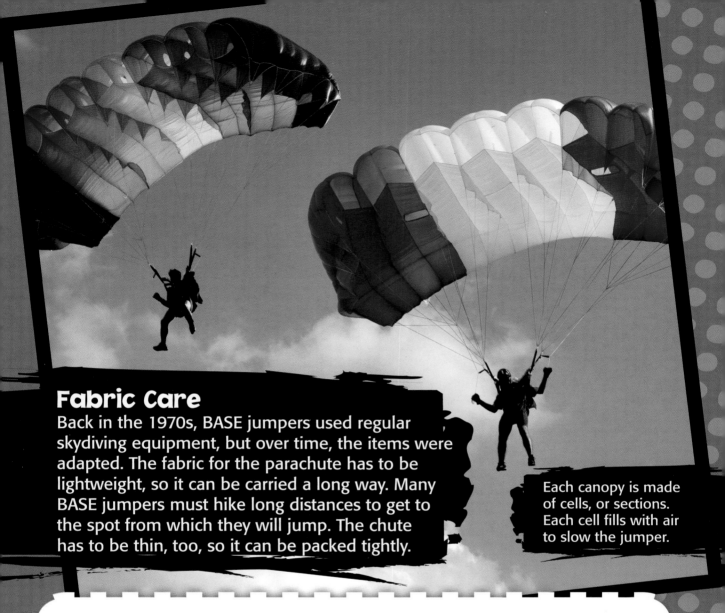

Fabric Care

Back in the 1970s, BASE jumpers used regular skydiving equipment, but over time, the items were adapted. The fabric for the parachute has to be lightweight, so it can be carried a long way. Many BASE jumpers must hike long distances to get to the spot from which they will jump. The chute has to be thin, too, so it can be packed tightly.

Each canopy is made of cells, or sections. Each cell fills with air to slow the jumper.

TEST IT!

To study the importance of the design of the chute, you can try making chutes of various materials, such as garbage bags and tissues. For each chute, tie or tape strings to the corners or edges, and hang a load from the strings. Use a heavy bolt or other small item as a weight for the chute to carry. See how well it flies, and then try changing your design. Consider these features and test each one of them.

☑ height of drop   ☑ weight of string

☑ shape of chute   ☑ height of string

☑ material of chute   ☑ weight of load

"Chute" the Breeze

Not all parachutes are created equal. Round parachutes are harder to control than long rectangles. BASE canopies and other parts are specially built. Like skydiving parachutes, some parachutes for BASE jumping have a second canopy, called a reserve. This is built into the parachute to work if all else fails. But for the shortest jumps, there is no time for a reserve.

The first BASE jumpers used round chutes, like those that were being used in skydiving. Today, even skydivers more often use the rectangular chutes.

Winging It

Some BASE jumpers wear **wingsuits**. These suits have flaps built into the arms and legs, which make it easier to glide but also harder to move the arms and legs. Wearing a wingsuit also makes it harder to control the canopy. The way the fall looks to someone in a wingsuit differs from how it looks to someone in a regular fall. When falling sideways in a suit, it is easier to mistake the distance to the landing site.

The larger the wings on the wingsuit, the more skill is needed to control the jump.

TEST IT!

Jumpers in wingsuits leap in a "head high" position, with arms wide out and legs closed. To figure out why, gather paper and pencil and draw a jumper in a wingsuit with his or her head high. Then, draw a jumper with head low. Draw arrows around the figures to represent **air flow** as the jumpers move downward. Draw arrows upward from the bottom of the page to represent the **air resistance**. It can be easier to think about these forces when using a diagram.

Pick a Pack

The chute has to open faster on a BASE jump than it does for skydiving. Instead of relying on a **rip cord**, BASE jumpers usually release their chutes by hand. The container system is what opens the canopy. It is important for BASE jumpers to have the newest container systems available. The updated gear is designed to make packing the parachute easier, and the containers are made to release the parachute faster and without risks.

The jumper tries to leap away from the object at the very start of the jump.

No Brainer

As in many extreme sports, BASE jumpers wear helmets to protect their heads. The jumpers also wear goggles, which can make it easier to see what is happening. This is one of the sports for which it makes no sense to borrow equipment or use something used. No one wants to be struggling with equipment in the middle of a jump.

In skydiving and especially in BASE jumping, the body's position is important. The jumper must face down, with the pack behind.

TEST IT!

When a parachute opens, it fills with air, which causes drag. The bigger the parachute, the more drag it creates. To see drag in action, float a paper plate down a tall stairway. Then, find out what happens when you tape a quarter to the middle. Next, try taping the coin to the edge. When the coin is at the edge, it tips the plate, which means there is less surface filling with air. The bigger the surface, the more drag it creates.

MASTERING THE JUMP

Experienced BASE jumpers are the only kind that there are. Before attempting a BASE jump, the jumper needs to go through many hours of skydiving. This develops canopy skills, which are the skills needed to control a parachute correctly. With the proper training, the jumps become safer, though they are never one hundred percent safe.

Asking someone for training is a huge request, because the trainer feels some responsibility for what happens.

Practice Is Priceless

To be ready for anything, the jumpers need training to be able to turn an open parachute almost as soon as the jump begins. This way, the jumpers can react if something is falling or flying through the air toward them. BASE jumpers also need special training for night jumps.

Many BASE jumpers discourage others from even trying this sport. They do not want to be responsible for the risk that someone else takes. The fact is, even the best jumpers cannot be sure their advice will help a new jumper. A person must jump in order to get the experience needed. To jump from dangerous spots, the person must jump often.

In a tandem jump, one person takes another along for a ride.

Sky Training

Making 200 or so skydives is the first step of training. During the first part of the process, jumpers become familiar with the tools of jumping. They learn about the dangers by making different kinds of jumps and dealing with the problems that arise. The hopeful BASE jumpers then look for a **mentor**. They try to find someone in the BASE community who can act as a guide.

Being able to steer away from the object being jumped from is a matter of skill and of life or death.

Of Course

New jumpers also take a course called First Jump Course, or FJC. There, they learn about the equipment and how to pack it. They find out how wind affects the jumps, and they investigate what makes a good landing area. Most of all, hopeful BASE jumpers study the things they can do if something goes wrong. They think through the actions they can take if, for instance, the chute opens to the left or right of where it should be.

Every detail matters, from packing the chute to checking the weather.

Go Local

In other countries, such as Australia and Canada, there are national BASE associations. In the United States, the groups tend to be local, and there are not many of them. BASE jumpers in the United States are more often part of a skydiving group.

U.S. skydiving groups include the United States Parachute Association and numerous state groups.

TEST IT!

As a jumper heads downward he or she gains speed. This increase is called acceleration. Some kind of force is needed to change the rate of acceleration. In other words, force is needed to speed it up, slow it down, or stop it. This fact is easily observed. Pushing a shopping cart takes a certain amount of force, and pushing it faster takes more force. How hard that force needs to be depends on the **mass** of the object in question.

Members of the Twin Falls BASE Association need to make ten jumps per year from the Perrine Bridge. Members need to live nearby as well.

Select Members

BASE jumpers in Twin Falls, Idaho, work to make sure that they can continue to jump from the Perrine Bridge. There are very few spots in the United States where BASE jumping is legal. Many people think it is too dangerous, and it has been outlawed in national parks. So the Twin Falls group tries to make sure that any news about BASE jumping is positive.

DAY TO REMEMBER

Recently, a BASE jumper from Russia traveled to a mountain in northern India. It took him 30 days to get where he was going, including a six-day climb up to the very top of the peak. It took him years of training and a month of travel to get to one big moment, when he broke a world record in 90 seconds.

Jumps from skyscrapers tend to range from 1,000 to 1,500 feet (305 to 457 m).

Record Breaker

The year was 2012. The BASE jumper was Valery Rozov. The mountain was Shivling, in the Himalayas. The jump was from 21,466 feet (6,543 m) high, the longest BASE jump ever.

Each record goes down in history as a name, a date and place, and some kind of measurement, but there is always a long story behind it all. The year before that record-breaking jump, the same diver jumped from a peak in Antarctica. The year before that, he jumped from a volcano in Russia.

Many BASE jumpers are world travelers. They go to the ends of Earth to test their skills.

Judging a Jump

BASE jumpers proudly share their highest jumps in all four categories. But like the athletes in many extreme sports, the jumpers mainly compete with themselves. It is all about setting goals and beating personal bests. They often try to keep their skills current by visiting new places, because having new experiences is another kind of thrill.

Some BASE jumpers try to break records for the number of jumpers to leap from one spot in a 24-hour period.

One to Four

In BASE jumping, it is hard to compare one person's record with another's, so the jumps that stand out are usually those that break a record. BASE 1 was awarded in 1981 to Phil Smith, of Houston, Texas. BASE 1,000 went to Matt Moilanen, from Kalamazoo, Michigan, in 2005. To earn a number any combination of building, antenna, span, and earth will work, so there are many combinations on record. People jump from smokestacks and dams. They leap from anything that is high enough. It is hard to judge a best overall, because the difficulty of each jump has many factors, including the weather.

In 1999, Felix Baumgartner jumped 95 feet (29 m) from a famous statue in Rio de Janeiro, Brazil. This was said to be a record for the world's shortest BASE jump. In BASE jumping, the shorter the jump, the more dangerous.

World Cup

To compete directly, BASE jumpers can take part in contests where their jumps are judged for speed or other factors. World associations offer world-class competitions. In 2012, the ProBASE World Cup had a showdown in Turkey and a competition in Greece. There was a wingsuit race in Switzerland and a track race in Norway. At the track race, the main goal was to leap the farthest at the start, when parallel to or level with the jump spot, and no wings were allowed. These events were all part of the ProBASE World Cup Tour. The best racer overall was crowned the champion.

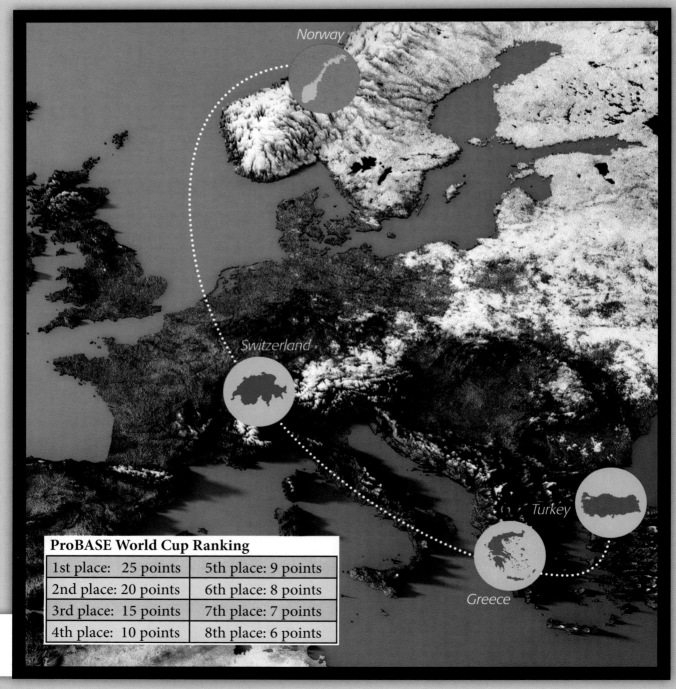

ProBASE World Cup Ranking	
1st place: 25 points	5th place: 9 points
2nd place: 20 points	6th place: 8 points
3rd place: 15 points	7th place: 7 points
4th place: 10 points	8th place: 6 points

Team USA

For the wingsuit competition, the fastest were selected, and then they competed with one another. Points were awarded for various reasons, such as the time it took for a jumper's canopy to open. Anyone who got in to someone else's lane was taken out of the race. Points were added up in all events.

The Jin Mao Tower in Shanghai, China, has been hosting BASE jumping events since 2003.

33

Newsmakers

Every BASE jumping event is filled with danger, and even the best in the sport get injured—or worse. One of the most famous people in the sport is Jeb Corliss. He was the first host of the TV show *Stunt Junkies*. There is also a movie about him called *Fearless: The Jeb Corliss Story*. His legs struck a rock ledge before he opened his chute. Corliss sustained major injuries to both legs.

Table Mountain is the national park in South Africa where Jeb Corliss was injured.

Fame Ends

Corliss had a close friend named Dwain Weston. Many people considered Weston the best BASE jumper ever. In 2003, both men jumped from an aircraft above the Royal Gorge Bridge in Colorado, to demonstrate how to fall close to objects. Weston was supposed to fly over the bridge but ended up crashing into a railing at 120 miles (193 m) per hour and did not survive.

BASE jumpers gather each September at the Royal Gorge Bridge for the Go Fast Games.

Attention Getting

In 2010, Nasr Al Niyadi and Omar Al Hegelan set a record for the highest jump from a building. They jumped from the Burj Khalifa in Dubai from a height of 2,205 feet (672 m). The story of their successful leap was featured by news outlets around the world. But there are also many horror stories about BASE jumpers. In 2011, for example, Christopher Brewer went to Bridge Day in West Virginia. His parachute did not work as it should have, and he had to make a landing with just his wingsuit to slow his fall. He hit the water at 80 miles (129 km) per hour. Brewer survived, but he was seriously injured.

The Burj Khalifa is the world's tallest building. The record-breaking BASE jumpers leaped from a platform on the 160th floor.

A Lift for Special Causes

Despite the accidents and dangers, BASE jumpers have been able to use their sport to attract positive attention to causes that they support. British BASE jumpers have tried to break records to raise money for war veterans. American BASE jumpers have collected pledges to raise money for kids with special needs.

A recent study determined that one in 60 BASE jumpers dies while practicing the sport.

LIVING THE DREAM

Can you imagine leaping off a cliff, strapped to a parachute? The place to begin is a skydiving center, where you can study with experts and earn a license to go skydiving. Then, you need to practice your skills for a year or longer. BASE jumping is not a sport you can jump in and start tomorrow.

After all these years, fewer than 2,000 people have applied for a BASE number.

Feel the Strength

Most people simply marvel at the jumps and the danger involved. But you can also take a lesson from these extreme athletes and the way that they train their bodies and throw themselves at their goals. To get fit, you can begin the strength training that helps BASE jumpers perform well.

TEST IT!

Beginning jumpers are often told to keep their chests pushed out to the horizon. This is because it is best to keep the body in balance during the jump. The spot on any body where weight sits in a balanced way is called the center of **gravity**. For most people, this is between the hips. Try finding the center of gravity on a baseball by balancing it on two fingers. You will see that the center of gravity is at the center of the ball.

Jumpers learn to feel their center of gravity, even as they fall.

Core Beliefs

Being strong throughout your **core** is important in this sport. Weight training and exercises such as squats and crunches strengthen the arms, legs, stomach, and sides. It also helps to run, because jumps so often start with a run.

Before BASE jumping, an athlete needs a long record of success in skydiving. Like any athletic skill, the preparation for a big jump takes thousands of hours.

Big Jump

In the James Bond movie *Die Another Day*, Bond jumps from an iceberg as if it were easy. In a popular video game, cartoon creatures BASE jump in a world of bright colors and explosions. In the real world, BASE jumping is as extreme as extreme sports get.

Whether jumping from the KL Tower in Malaysia, or the big bridge in Fayetteville, West Virginia, BASE jumping requires some serious skills.

BASE means life on the edge!

BASE jumpers apply to be among the few people allowed to jump from Kuala Lumpur Tower, or KL Tower, at night.

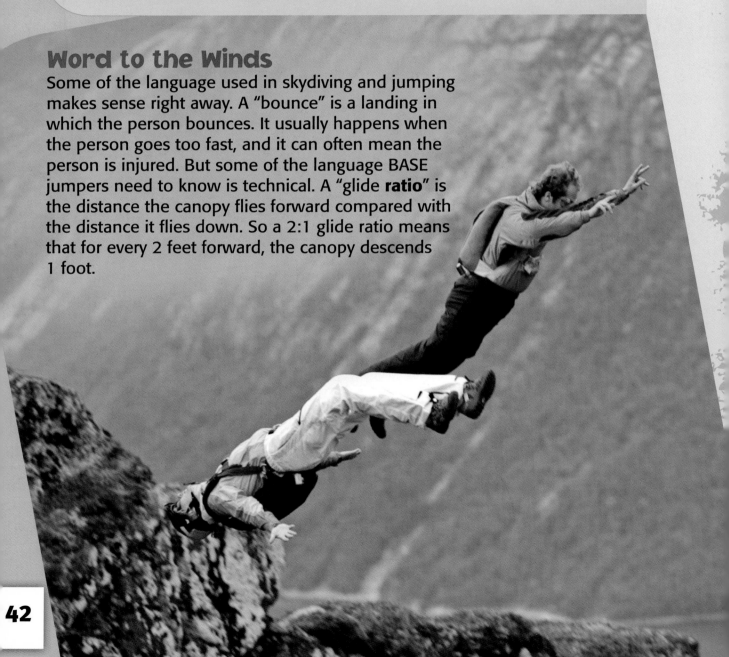

JUMP ON JARGON

To be a BASE jumper, you need to know skydiving, and to understand skydiving, you need to know the language of the sport. One thing you do not want to be called is a *jump wonder*. That is someone who thinks too much of his or her own skills.

Word to the Winds

Some of the language used in skydiving and jumping makes sense right away. A "bounce" is a landing in which the person bounces. It usually happens when the person goes too fast, and it can often mean the person is injured. But some of the language BASE jumpers need to know is technical. A "glide **ratio**" is the distance the canopy flies forward compared with the distance it flies down. So a 2:1 glide ratio means that for every 2 feet forward, the canopy descends 1 foot.

Words in Context

Can you guess the meaning of these skydiving words and phrases?

1. We had a *boogie* on the bridge on Memorial Day weekend. It was really something to see.

   boogie: gathering of divers

2. I'll meet you at the *drop zone*.

   drop zone: center for skydiving or BASE jumping

3. He is such a *wuffo*. My whole family is, except me.

   wuffo: someone who will not jump and does not understand it

LEGENDS OF BASE JUMPING

The legends of BASE jumping are men and women whose skills and daring stand out even among BASE jumpers. They attempted and were successful at extreme tests of BASE skills. Here are a few of the record breakers.

Five Famous BASE Jumpers

In 2006, **Captain Daniel G. Schilling** jumped from the Perrine Bridge in Twin Falls, Idaho, 201 times in 24 hours. According to Guinness World Records, this is the most jumps in 24 hours.

In 2006, **Glenn Singleman** and **Heather Swan** jumped from Mount Meru in India. They leaped from the **altitude** of 21,666 feet (6,604 m), which broke the record for highest altitude at the time.

In 2010, **Nasr Al Niyadi** and **Omar Al Hegelan** jumped 2,204 feet 8 inches (672 m) from the Burj Khalifa in the United Arab Emirates. This is the highest jump from a building on record.

Behind the Legends

Among the legends of BASE jumping are the pioneers of this extreme sport. Here are three that are recognized by ProBASE for the difference they made in the way that BASE jumping caught on.

name	country	accomplishments
Carl Boenish	United States	invented the BASE name, developed special gear, held the record for the highest BASE jump in his time
Dwain Weston	Australia	remembered for performing tricky feats while in the air, widely recognized as best in the sport until his death during a stunt
Roland "Slim" Simpson	Australia	first to reach the 1,000 jump mark, worked to make BASE jumping legal and to start BASE competitions

BASE Knowledge

To become an expert in BASE jumping, you can dive into this list of famous BASE jumping spots. Use your library, and the Internet, to research why they are so popular. Find out where the spots are located and whether they are a building, an antenna, a span, or a structure of earth. Learn about their heights and other features.

Destination	Country
El Capitan	United States
Troll Wall	Norway
Angel Falls	Venezuela
Trango Towers	Pakistan
New River Gorge Bridge	United States
Kjerag	Norway
Perrine Bridge	United States

Glossary

air flow: motion of air currents around a moving object

air resistance: force that works against forward movement in air

altitude: measure of space above a surface; height

antenna: a wire or rod that sends and receives electrical signals

canopy: rooflike covering, such as the fabric part of a parachute

core: on a human body, the trunk, or body minus arms, legs, and head

drag: force that fights or slows movement through air or through fluids such as water

fixed object: object that is attached and stays in place

gorge: narrow passage through land with steep walls

gravity: attraction between objects that have mass

mass: the amount of matter in an object

mentor: trusted guide or support person

parachutes: devices for slowing downward movement that consist of canopies attached to bodies by cords

pyramid: figure with triangles for sides

ratio: relation between two values, such as numbers or measures

rip cord: cord that is pulled to release a parachute

span: in BASE, a bridge; in general, the distance between two ends

wingsuits: suits with flaps below arms and between legs

For More Information

Books

Cefrey, Holly. *Skysurfing.* New York, NY: Childrens Press, 2003.

Hollihan, Kerrie Logan. *Isaac Newton and Physics for Kids.* Chicago, IL.: Chicago Review Press, 2009.

Krull, Kathleen. *Isaac Newton.* New York, NY: Viking, 2006.

Schindler, John E. *Hang Gliding and Parasailing (Extreme Sports).* Milwaukee, WI.: Gareth Stevens, 2005.

Websites

Bridge Day
www.officialbridgeday.com/base-jumping

The official site for Bridge Day in Fayetteville, West Virginia, includes a photo gallery of BASE jumpers in action. It also explains the rules for admission.

How Wingsuit Flying Works
adventure.howstuffworks.com/wingsuit-flying.htm

This How Stuff Works article includes video of a diver in a wingsuit. It outlines the way the wingsuit works and explains much of the science behind its design.

Index

air flow 19
Al Hegelan, Omar 36, 44
Al Niyadi, Nasr 36, 44
altitude 44
Angel Falls 8, 45
antenna 7, 11, 31, 45
associations 26, 32

Baumgartner, Felix 31
Boenish, Carl 11, 12, 13, 45
Brewer, Christopher 36
Bridge Day 4, 6, 9, 36, 47
Burj Khalifa 36, 44

canopy 16, 18, 19, 22, 33, 42
cells 17
CN Tower 12
container 20
Corliss, Jeb 34, 35

da Vinci, Leonardo 10
drag 16, 21

Eiffel Tower 13
El Capitan 13, 45
Eustace, Bill 13

First Jump Course (FJC) 25
fixed object 7

Garnerin, André-Jacques 13
Gateway Arch 9
goggles 21
gravity 39

Himalayas 5, 29

Kjerag 8, 45
KL Tower 41

Lenormand, Louis-Sébastian 13

mass 26
mentor 24
Moilanen, Matt 31

New River Gorge Bridge 4, 45

Perrine Bridge 27, 44, 45
ProBASE 32, 45

reserve 18
rip cord 20
Royal Gorge Bridge 35
Rozov, Valery 28, 29

Schilling, Daniel G. 44
Shivling 29
Singleman, Glenn 44
skydiving 7, 12, 14, 15, 17, 18, 20, 21, 22, 24, 26, 38, 40, 42, 43, 47
Smith, Phil 11, 31
span 7, 11, 31, 45
Stunt Junkies 34
Swan, Heather 44
Sylvester, Rick 13

Table Mountain 34
Trango Towers 45
Twin Falls 27, 44

United States Parachute Association 26

Weston, Dwain 35, 44
wingsuits 19, 32, 33, 47

Yosemite 12